May 18

♡ The Wildwood Bakery ♡

Read more
OWL DIARIES
books!

OWL DIARIES

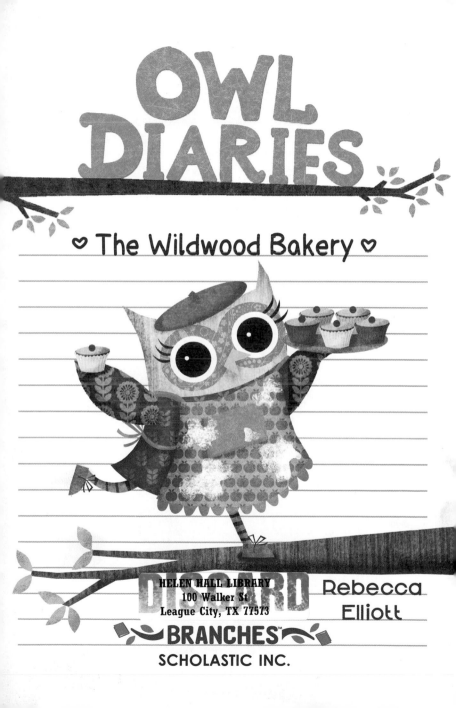

♡ The Wildwood Bakery ♡

Rebecca Elliott

BRANCHES

SCHOLASTIC INC.

For Maisy and Katie, who have the
coolest wingchairs around.—R.E.

Special thanks to Eva Montgomery.

Copyright © 2017 by Rebecca Elliott

All rights reserved. Published by Scholastic Inc., *Publishers since 1920.*
SCHOLASTIC, BRANCHES, and associated logos are trademarks
and/or registered trademarks of Scholastic Inc.

The publisher does not have any control over and does not assume
any responsibility for author or third-party websites or their content.

No part of this publication may be reproduced, stored in a retrieval system,
or transmitted in any form or by any means, electronic, mechanical,
photocopying, recording, or otherwise, without written permission of the
publisher. For information regarding permission, write to Scholastic Inc.,
Attention: Permissions Department, 557 Broadway, New York, NY 10012.

This book is a work of fiction. Names, characters, places, and incidents are
either the product of the author's imagination or are used fictitiously, and any
resemblance to actual persons, living or dead, business establishments,
events, or locales is entirely coincidental.

Library of Congress Cataloging-in-Publication Data
Names: Elliott, Rebecca, author. I Elliott, Rebecca. Owl diaries ; 7.
Title: The Wildwood Bakery / Rebecca Elliott.
Description: First edition. I New York : Branches/Scholastic Inc., 2017. I
Series: Owl diaries ; 7 I Summary: Macy's little sister has wings that are
too small, so Eva's class decides to raise money to buy her a flying
chair, and half the class opens a bakery, and the other half opens a candy
store—but soon competition between the two stores becomes more important
than their goal, and Eva needs to convince the other owls that they will
collect more money if everyone works as a team.
Identifiers: LCCN 2017015799 I ISBN 9781338163001 (pbk.) I ISBN 9781338163018
(hardcover)
Subjects: LCSH: Owls–Juvenile fiction. I Elementary schools–Juvenile
fiction. I Money-making projects for children–Juvenile fiction. I
Bakeries–Juvenile fiction. I Cooperativeness–Juvenile fiction. I
Diaries–Juvenile fiction. I CYAC: Owls–Fiction. I Schools–Fiction. I
Fund raising–Fiction. I Bakers and bakeries–Fiction. I
Cooperativeness–Fiction. I Diaries–Fiction.
Classification: LCC PZ7.E45812 Wi 2017 I DDC [Fic]–dc23 LC record available at https://
lccn.loc.gov/2017015799

10 9 8 7 6 5 4 3 2 1   17 18 19 20 21

Printed in China   38
First edition, November 2017

Book design by Marissa Asuncion
Edited by Katie Carella

♡ Table of Contents ♡

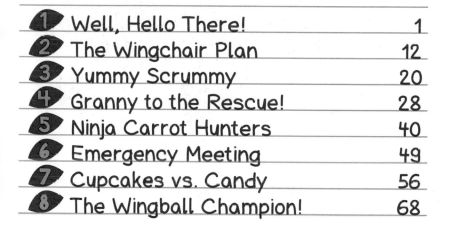

1 Well, Hello There!   1
2 The Wingchair Plan   12
3 Yummy Scrummy   20
4 Granny to the Rescue!   28
5 Ninja Carrot Hunters   40
6 Emergency Meeting   49
7 Cupcakes vs. Candy   56
8 The Wingball Champion!   68

11

Woodpine Avenue

♡ Well, Hello There! ♡

Sunday

Hello Diary,
    Did you miss me? It's me — Eva
Wingdale! I wonder what exciting
adventure we'll have this week!

<u>I love</u>:

Granny Owlberta's
cookies

The word
<u>bubble</u>

<u>Saving up my
moon dollars</u>

Funny jokes

Squirrels

HA HA!

Baby Mo's
laugh

Helping others

Winning at
WINGBALL

3

I DO NOT love:

Stinky cheese

Rain clouds

WAA WAA!

Baby Mo's cry

Cleaning
my room

4

Washing my wings
before I eat

The word gray

Mom's slug stew

Losing at
WINGBALL

My family is **FLAPERIFFIC**!

Here is a picture of us on Warm Hearts Day:

Mom

Dad

Me   Baby Mo

Humphrey

We all love Baxter – my cute pet bat.

I'm so lucky to be an owl. Owls do the best stuff...

We are awake when the sun has gone to bed.

We fly like superheroes.

We make super loud <u>hoot</u> sounds.

HOOT!

And we hatch out of eggs when we're chicks!

This is my tree house.

I live next door to my best friend EVER, Lucy Beakman. We sit together in Mrs. Featherbottom's class.

10

Here is our class photo:

I can't wait to see all my friends at school tomorrow! Better get some sleep. Good day, Diary!

♡The Wingchair Plan♡

Monday

Today, Mrs. Featherbottom asked us each to share something we did over the weekend.

I played cards with Granny Owlberta and Grandpa Owlfred.

I made a model of the Owlpire State Building!

I read the new Owl Ninja book.

I practiced playing my owlaphone.

I went to Brown Bear Mall with my little sister, Mia. We bought her a school bag.

Just then, I had a **FLAP-TASTIC** idea!

We could all raise the money for Mia's wingchair!

Eva, that's a splendid idea!

Class, your homework tonight is to think of the best fund-raising idea!

After school, Lucy came over, and we baked cookies.

Then I had ANOTHER **FLAP-TASTIC** IDEA — and so did Lucy! Both at the same time!

I'm SO excited! I can't wait to tell everyone our idea tomorrow!

3

♡ Yummy Scrummy ♡

Tuesday

School was such a **HOOT** today, Diary! Mrs. Featherbottom asked us to share our fund-raising ideas.

Everyone pays one moon dollar to wear pajamas to school!

We could sell our paintings!

A stay-awake-a-thon!

A magic show!

We all cheered.

At lunch, we sat in our groups.

It took us AGES to come up with a name . . .

Next, we made a list of everything we need to do before Saturday:

1. Design our shop sign
2. Make flyers to advertise the shop
3. Bake cookies to sell
4. Decorate shop bags
5. Make garlands for inside the shop

After school, we went to my tree house to bake. But the cookie batter didn't taste good. So we used it for a food fight instead!

We'll have to bake FOR REAL tomorrow...

♥ Granny to the Rescue! ♥

Wednesday

Diary, sometimes Sue can be nice and sometimes Sue can be, well, Sue. Today, Sue was being Sue.

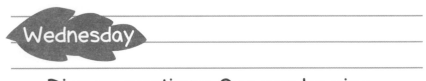

We're going to sell SO MANY of our super-tasty candies. No one will have any money left to spend at your bakery.

Don't be so sure, Sue. Our cookies are going to be BIG sellers, too.

During class, both teams worked on shop signs. Zac came up with ours.

We copied it to make our Wildwood Bakers membership cards.

At recess, I called our first secret Wildwood Bakers meeting. Everyone showed their cards and said the password. It was such a **HOOT**!

Everyone looked at me like I was crazy.

Later, we told Granny Owlberta and Grandpa Owlfred about our shop.

I'd love to help you raise money for Mia's special wingchair! And I have a <u>wing-tastic</u> recipe for cookies! I can teach it to you now, if you'd like?

That would be owlmazing!

Thank you!

We baked YUMMY cookies.

Then Hailey thought she saw someone at the window.

We flew outside.

No one was there. But Macy found something.

We flew back inside.

I bet they're trying to steal our ideas!

We HAVE to raise more money than them!

Yes, we have to win!

Calm down, owlets. Try not to worry about what other owls are doing. Just do your best. That's all any of us can do.

Granny is a very wise old owl. In order to do our BEST though, we'll need more than a cookie recipe.

Dreamy Creamy Carrot Cupcakes

1 cup sugar
1 cup flour
6 bugs
2 acorns
1 cup wild carrots

- Mix together the
  first 4 ingredients
- Shred the carrots
  and stir them in
- Pour batter into muffin pan
- Bake for 30 minutes
- Let cupcakes cool
- Put loads of icing on top
- Enjoy!

Then Granny whispered:

Hard. But not impossible. It's too late tonight but . . . when you can, follow the rabbits. Just don't let them see you because they won't like you taking their carrots! Dress in dark clothes to stay hidden.

Everyone said good-bye to Granny and Grandpa. Then we all flew home.

Diary, tomorrow we are going to find those wild carrots and bake those Dreamy Creamies! It's the ONLY way we'll win.

♡ Ninja Carrot Hunters ♡

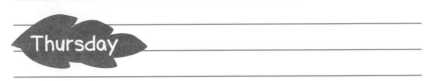
Thursday

When we got to school, everyone was whispering about secret plans for the shops. Sue was listening in on us. Again. It made me a bit mad.

I know you were spying on us last night, Sue!

Don't be silly, Eva. Why would I do that? We have the very best ideas for our shop.

Well, we have a top-secret recipe now. So our shop is definitely going to win!

We'll just see about that!

Mrs. Featherbottom called Sue and me over to her desk.

Now, girls, let's remember the most important thing is that your shops are raising money for Macy's little sister, Mia, and her special chair. I don't want to hear any more talk about winning.

I knew Mrs. Featherbottom was right. But I also still REALLY wanted our shop to raise more money than Sue's.

I called another secret Wildwood Bakers meeting.

We have to raise as much money as possible. That means we have to bake those Dreamy Creamies!

We need to find those carrots!

Meet at my tree house after school. And remember: Wear dark clothes!

We should dress up like ninjas!

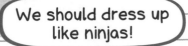

When the Wildwood Bakers met up, we all looked so cool!

We really do look like ninjas!

Ninja carrot hunters!

Come on! Let's find a rabbit to follow!

We flew around the forest looking for a rabbit.

We followed the rabbit to a patch of wild carrots. We hid in a tree and kept really quiet.

What now? Do we just take their carrots?

Those are <u>wild</u> carrots — they don't belong to the rabbits.

But still . . . We should ask before taking them.

I'll go talk to the rabbits. Wait here.

My friends flew down, and we picked
wild carrots together.

Back at my tree house, we baked the
Dreamy Creamies.

We baked SO MANY that we used up
all our sugar!

Dad was our first taste tester.

These cupcakes are flaperrific! Can I have another?

I think you've had enough.

Granny did say that one is never enough!

Oh, go on then. But only if I can have one, too!

Diary, my bedroom is FILLED with cookies and cupcakes. YUM!

♥ Emergency Meeting ♥

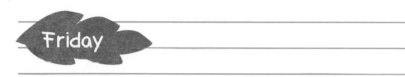

Friday

Hi Diary,
    I cannot believe it's already Friday!
Our shop opens tomorrow!!

At recess today, we had fun playing **WINGBALL**. But the nets, uniforms, and balls are so old they're falling apart.

Our school <u>really</u> needs new wingball stuff!

I know, and it's too bad because my little sister loves wingball. It's one of the reasons she is looking forward to starting school.

After school, we worked hard.

Lucy and I made the garlands.

Zac and Hailey made the flyers.

George, Macy, and Mia decorated the bags. (We were lucky Mia helped out!)

Thanks so much, Mia!

You're great at this!

I love to draw!

We got everything ready in no time.

Next, we flew around the forest.
We left a flyer on every doorstep so
EVERYONE would know about our
shop.

I can't wait for tomorrow!

Cupcakes vs. Candy

Saturday

We flew to the Old Oak Tree super early. We decorated our shop and put out the cupcakes and cookies.

Customers were lined up outside. Our families and friends and neighbors were all there!

Finally, it was
time to open the shop.

Oh my, Diary! Running
a bakery is hard work . . .

We had to get the cupcakes and
cookies for everyone.

We had to bag
them up.

And we had
to charge the
right amount of
moon dollars.

I took a quick peek at Candy Crunch Corner. Sue's shop seemed to have just as many owls in it as ours. So I wasn't sure who was winning.

At the end of the night, we were closing up when . . .

DISASTER!!!

We huddled together.

Everyone was quiet. We were all thinking hard about this decision.

> If borrowing sugar helps us raise more money and win, then we should do it!

We flew to Candy Crunch Corner. Sue's team was all in a **FLAP** – just like we were!

Just then, we heard Mia's voice behind us.

I don't think I want a wingchair anymore. I thought these shops were supposed to be a fun way to help me. But the two teams aren't even friends anymore, and all you guys seem to want to do is win.

Everyone felt bad. We had forgotten why we were doing this in the first place. We had also forgotten we were all friends. And friends help one another.

Mrs. Featherbottom came to see how our shops had done in their first night. She counted up the moon dollars.

Both shops did very well — SO well that we have already raised enough money for Mia's wingchair!

Wow!

That's owlmazing! Thank you so much, everyone!

Mia and her Dad flew off.

We're so thankful to you all. Mia, let's go buy your new wingchair!

We told Mrs. Featherbottom our plan to put both shops together. She loved it!

We all flew to Sue's house to bake. We had a **FLAPERRIFIC** time!

When I got home, Humphrey burst into my room.

How's the bakery, Eva? Save any treats for me?

I did actually. Here you go.

Oh no!

What is it?

I forgot to take cupcakes to the rabbits who gave us the carrots!

So, Diary, I've set my alarm for super early tomorrow. I'm so tired . . .

♡ The Wingball Champion! ♡

Sunday

I flew to the rabbits' carrot patch when it was still light.

The new Wildcandy Cake Shop was a big success tonight! We had so much fun working together! After we closed up our shop, we ate the leftover treats.

Then Mia flew — yes, FLEW — in on her new wingchair!

I'm so proud of all of you. And . . . Surprise! The school is going to use the money you raised tonight to buy new wingball nets, balls, and uniforms!

I bought one new ball already! Mia, catch!

The ball flew through the air.

Mia swooped up to catch it. She moved faster than any owl I've ever seen!

Wow, Mia!

It looks like the Treetop Owlementary wingball team has a new star player!

We all cheered! This was such a great week, Diary. See you next time!

Rebecca Elliott was a lot like Eva when she was younger: She loved making things and hanging out with her best friends. Now that Rebecca is older, not much has changed — except that her best friends are her husband, Matthew, and their children. She still loves making things, like stories, cakes, music, and paintings. But as much as she and Eva have in common, Rebecca cannot fly or turn her head all the way around. No matter how hard she tries.

Rebecca is the author of JUST BECAUSE and MR. SUPER POOPY PANTS. OWL DIARIES is her first early chapter book series.

OWL DIARIES

How much do you know about The Wildwood Bakery?

What is a <u>wingchair</u>? How is it similar to a <u>wheelchair</u>? Why does Mia need one?

Look at page 43. Why are the Wildwood Bakers dressed like ninjas?

What is the disaster that happens at the end of the Wildwood Bakery's first night?

Mia uses a special wingchair to fly. Do you know anyone who uses something special to help them?

How is the Wildcandy Cake Shop formed? Use details to describe the thoughts, feelings, and actions of Eva and her classmates.

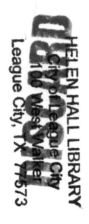